A CHRISTMAS CAROL

Original story by Charles Dickens

Retold by Margaret McAllister

Series Editor Professor Kimberley Reynolds

Illustrated by Pete Williamson

OXFORD
UNIVERSITY PRESS

Letter from the Author

One Christmas Eve when I was young, in a house where the television was a small box with pictures in black, white and grey and the fireplace had a proper fire with real coals, I was watching a film. A face appeared in a door knocker. Ghostly feet in chains clanked  upstairs. I was fascinated. The film was *A Christmas Carol*, and I couldn't wait to read the book. *A Christmas Carol* has everything – exciting stuff, funny stuff, sad and sweet stuff, great characters and a perfect ending. And snow!

I was always reading. If I didn't have a book in my hands, I was either asleep or getting the cat out of a tree. Of all the books I've read, *A Christmas Carol* is still a favourite. I hope you love this book so much that one day you'll do what I did, and go on to read the original version.

Margaret McAllister

Chapter One

Marley was dead. You must understand that Marley was dead, or this story will not surprise you at all. The names 'Scrooge and Marley' were still over the office door, but only Marley's business partner Ebenezer Scrooge remained. Scrooge was a harsh, thin man with a cold heart, and cared only for making money and keeping it.

On a dark Christmas Eve in London, Scrooge was at work in his chilly office. The next room, where his clerk Bob Cratchit worked, was colder still. Poor Bob didn't dare put more coal on the fire. He tried to warm his hands at the candle instead.

'Merry Christmas, Uncle!' called a cheerful voice from the door. In walked Scrooge's nephew Fred, a bright-eyed, smiling young man.

'Christmas!' retorted Scrooge. 'Bah! Humbug! What's merry about it? You're a year older and no richer! Every fool who goes around wishing "Merry Christmas" should be boiled with the pudding and buried with holly through his heart. Humbug! What good does it do you?'

'Good?' repeated Fred. 'Of course it does good! At Christmas people are kind and think of others. Uncle, my wife and I would like you to come to us for Christmas dinner tomorrow!'

'Good afternoon!' snapped Scrooge, meaning 'Certainly not!' and 'Out!' at the same time.

Away went Fred, stopping to wish Bob a
Merry Christmas. As he left, two gentlemen
came into the office. Scrooge scowled.

'We're collecting money to help the poor
and distressed, who go cold and hungry in
winter,' explained one of them. 'Would you
make a donation?'

'Are there no prisons?' demanded
Scrooge. 'No workhouses?'

'There are,' said the gentleman. 'But many would rather die than go there.'

'Then let them die,' said Scrooge. 'Good afternoon!'

Finally, long after dark, Scrooge closed his account book and put on his hat.

'I suppose I have to give you all of Christmas Day off, Bob Cratchit,' he growled. 'So get here all the earlier next morning!'

Bob ran home gladly to his family, and Scrooge trudged to his rooms in a tall, dismal house. His key was in the lock when he noticed the door knocker.

But it was *not* the door knocker. It was Jacob Marley's face. And *Marley was dead!*

The next moment, it was a door knocker again. Scrooge stared, then pulled himself together, let himself in and mounted the dark, cold stairs to his dreary rooms. There, he locked the door and sat down to a bowl of gruel before bed. The fire was low and the light dim. Scrooge tried hard not to think about that door knocker and Jacob Marley's face.

A bell hanging in a corner of the room began, slowly, to ring. From all over the house bells rang, chimed, clanged – then all stopped together.

Into that silence came a noise like the dragging of heavy chains down in the cellars. A door banged open. Something dragged and clanked up the stairs, nearer and nearer ...

'Humbug!' muttered Scrooge.

Chapter Two

At that moment, Jacob Marley walked through the wall.

It certainly was Marley, though Scrooge could see through him. The chain he dragged was loaded down with steel money boxes, purses, locks and keys, and his eyes were deathly cold.

'Jacob!' cried Scrooge. 'Why are you here?'

'When I lived, I should have cared about people and gone among them,' groaned Marley. 'I did not, so I must do it now. My chain is made of money boxes and purses because that is all I thought about. Ebenezer! You are far worse than I was! You too will become a restless ghost, unless you change! Tonight, three spirits will visit you.'

'I'd rather they didn't,' pleaded Scrooge.

'Only they can help you to change!' cried Marley. 'Learn from them!'

The ghost stepped out of the window and into the air. Scrooge collapsed on his bed.

One o'clock struck. Scrooge woke as light filled the room. Near his bed stood a strange figure as small and smooth-skinned as a child, but with long white hair and a wise old face.

The figure carried a holly branch, and light poured from its head. 'I am the Spirit of Christmas Past,' it said quietly. '*Your* past. Come with me!'

Scrooge felt it was much too cold to go anywhere and he should stay in bed, but the Spirit led him across the room and through the wall.

Scrooge found himself by a country road on a crisp snowy day.

'I remember this place!' he cried. 'My school was here!'

Carts rumbled past, filled with schoolboys and their luggage. The boys laughed, waved, and wished each other Merry Christmas.

'They can't see you,' said the Spirit. 'Come!'

Scrooge followed the Spirit to a big, lonely school. His old school. Memories of it caused a tear to trickle slowly down his face.

'One child is still here, isn't he?' said the Spirit, gently. They stepped into a bare room where a boy sat reading by the fire. 'He can't go home for Christmas.'

'That's me,' muttered Scrooge.

'Now let's look at another Christmas!' announced the Spirit.

Now the same boy sat in the same place, but older. When a little girl ran in and hugged him he brightened up at once.

'I've come to take you home!' she cried. 'Father is much kinder now, and home is heaven! I asked if you could come home for Christmas, and he wants you to come for good! We're going home!'

'My dear sister Fan!' exclaimed Scrooge in delight. 'She grew up and had a son, my nephew Fred, but she died.'

'And *another* Christmas!' proclaimed the Spirit. The scene changed to Christmas Eve in a busy office.

'I worked here when I was young!' smiled Scrooge. 'It's Fezziwig's! There he is!'

A plump, jolly man at a desk looked at the clock, laid down his pen, and laughed.

'Time for the Christmas party!' he called. 'Stop work!'

Scrooge watched his younger self as everyone hurried to prepare the party. Mr Fezziwig's round, smiling wife and three round, smiling daughters appeared, ready to dance.

Friends and neighbours arrived and everyone threw themselves merrily into dancing and games. As Scrooge watched, he remembered it vividly and enjoyed it all over again.

'What a good man Fezziwig was!' Scrooge said. 'So generous to everyone who worked for him! Seeing him makes me wish I had been kinder to Bob Cratchit yesterday.'

'I must go soon,' said the Spirit. 'One more Christmas.'

The party scene vanished. Scrooge saw himself as a young man, with a pretty girl.

'It's hopeless,' she was saying tearfully. 'When we met we were both poor and we didn't mind. Now you don't love me, you only love money. I can't marry you!'

'Spirit!' groaned Scrooge. 'Why do you torment me?'

But there was no answer. Scrooge was in his room again, and in bed.

Chapter Three

Scrooge fell asleep, and woke again to see a warm glow of light. Nervously, he sat up.

Astonishing! The whole room was so glorious with holly, ivy and mistletoe that it looked like a forest! A log fire blazed merrily in the hearth.

On the floor Christmas puddings, pies, fruit and nuts were heaped up to make a throne for a huge, smiling figure. He wore a green robe trimmed with white, a holly wreath was on his head, and he held up a fiery torch.

'Come here and know me better!' he cried. 'I am the Spirit of Christmas Present!'

'Spirit,' said Scrooge shyly, 'I learned much from the first Spirit. I am ready to learn again.'

'Then touch my robe!' commanded the Spirit. Scrooge did, and the Spirit led him through bustling streets to the small house where Bob Cratchit lived.

There was such excitement in the Cratchit house!

All were in their
best clothes,
though
even these
were old and
mended.
In came young
Martha Cratchit
straight from
work, and
at last Bob
arrived
with
a small
child on his
shoulders. The child carried a crutch.

'Here's Father and Tiny Tim!' cried the
children, and soon the family were seated at
the table with Tiny Tim beside Bob.

How they all gasped with delight at
the sight and smell and taste of the roast
goose! How they praised Mrs Cratchit for
the excellent Christmas pudding! It seemed
a small pudding for a large family, but
everyone was happy.

'Merry Christmas!' called Tiny Tim.
'God bless us, every one!'

As they gathered round the fire after dinner, Bob kept Tim close to him, holding his hand. Scrooge observed how frail the child looked.

'Spirit,' he asked, 'will he die?'

'He will,' said the Spirit, 'if nothing changes. Today you were asked to help the poor. Do you remember your answer? You said, "Let them die."'

Now the Spirit whisked Scrooge away
to the home of Scrooge's nephew Fred, and
his wife. A splendid party was happening!
As Scrooge and the Spirit arrived,
everyone was laughing.

'He said Christmas was a humbug!'
laughed Fred. 'Poor Uncle Scrooge! I still
invite him every year.'

They played games, danced, and
sang, and Scrooge found it wonderfully
entertaining. He watched the dancing,
laughed at the games, and guessed the
riddles. He was still enjoying it when the
Spirit whisked him away to a barren,
lonely place.

Solemnly, the Spirit held out his robe. To Scrooge's horror two scrawny children huddled beneath it, thin, dirty, and scowling with hatred. They looked nothing like normal children – no, they were terrifying.

'These children belong to all people,' explained the Spirit. 'The girl is Hunger, and the boy is Ignorance. Beware them, especially the boy! Ignorance is deadly!'

'Have they no homes?' asked Scrooge.

'Are there no prisons?' demanded the Spirit in Scrooge's own words. 'No workhouses?'

But now, Scrooge could no longer see the Spirit of Christmas Present. Another ghost was approaching him.

Chapter Four

The tall figure was draped in black and Scrooge could see no face, only an outstretched hand. Terrified, he fell to his knees.

'Spirit of Christmas Yet to Come!' Scrooge cried. 'I mean to change my way of life! Help me!'

The Spirit said nothing but only led the way ahead, and Scrooge seemed to be carried along behind him.

They reached the city, where a group of businessmen were discussing somebody who had recently died.

'He won't be missed,' said one.

'It'll be a cheap funeral,' said another. 'Nobody will go.'

Scrooge wanted to know who they meant, but the silent Spirit led him away and down the filthiest, darkest, most tumbledown alley Scrooge had ever seen.

At a dirty little junk shop, a few men and women crouched over bundles. One was trying to sell blankets, another teaspoons, and another a long white shirt.

'They dressed him in this shirt to bury him,' she cackled. 'What a waste! He never did any good in his life. We may as well get something from his death.'

'Who do they mean?' asked Scrooge.

At once the Spirit took him to a dark, bare room where a figure lay on the bed, covered by a sheet. The Spirit pointed.

'Is this the dead man?' asked Scrooge. 'Spirit, I dare not look at him! Take me away from this place!'

The scene changed again. Now it was another Christmas at Bob Cratchit's house, but there was no merriment. The family sat quietly round the fire, but somebody was missing.

'Poor Tiny Tim,' sighed Bob. 'None of us will ever forget him. I saw Mr Scrooge's nephew Fred in town today and he said he was heartily sorry to hear about our Tim. What a kind gentleman!'

Wretchedly, Scrooge turned to the Spirit. 'Tell me, Spirit,' he said. 'Who was the man on the bed, the one they talked about?' He found himself in a neglected and overgrown churchyard. Silently, the Spirit pointed to a tombstone. Scrooge trembled as he bent to read the name on it.

'Spirit!' he cried, snatching the Spirit's hand. 'May these things not happen! I am a changed man! I promise to keep Christmas with all my heart!'

Ebenezer Scrooge

Chapter Five

Before Scrooge's eyes, the Spirit shrank and seemed to become a bedpost. And it really was a bedpost! Scrooge was in bed and the bells were ringing out on a glorious Christmas morning.

'I'm alive!' he cried in delight. 'It's Christmas, and my life is ahead of me! Thank you, Jacob Marley! Thank you, Spirits!'

He jumped out of bed and tried to dress himself, but he was too excited. He mixed up his clothes and found he was putting them on back to front, so he gave up and for the first time in years he laughed, long and loudly. Still in his nightshirt, he threw open the window.

A small boy was playing in the snow outside. Scrooge sent him on an errand to the butcher's shop and arranged to have the biggest turkey in the shop sent to the Cratchits. He rewarded the boy and the butcher generously, and laughed again.

'Bob won't know who sent it!' he said, dancing with glee.

When he had calmed himself he dressed
and walked out into the crisp cold morning,
wishing a Merry Christmas to passers-by.
Everything he did, singing carols in church,
watching the happiness of people in the
street, everything gave him joy. At last, shyly,
he called at Fred's house.

'Fred,' he asked, 'may I join you for
Christmas?'

May he? Fred shook Scrooge by the hand
as if he would never let go! Scrooge was
made so welcome that in no time at all he
felt completely at home. Guests arrived,
dancing began, and it was the happiest
gathering Scrooge had been to in many,
many years.

Even so, he was at the office early next morning, crouched over his desk. He was planning a surprise. To his delight, Bob Cratchit arrived nearly twenty minutes late.

'You're late!' snarled Scrooge. 'And I'll tell you what I'm going to do about it!'

He leaped to his feet. Bob stepped back in alarm. 'I'm going to raise your salary!' laughed Scrooge.

Bob suspected that Scrooge had gone mad. He backed away, ready to run into the street and shout for help.

'Merry Christmas, Bob!' said Scrooge, patting him on the back. 'Don't be afraid! I have come to my senses! Let's heap coal on the fire, then have some hot punch and discuss how I can help your family!'

Scrooge lived happily and generously for the rest of his life. He helped Bob's family and was like a second father to Tiny Tim, who did *not* die. People said that Scrooge knew how to keep Christmas better than anyone. And as Tiny Tim said, 'God bless us, every one!'

About Charles Dickens

Charles Dickens was born on 7 February 1812, during a time called the Industrial Revolution. More and bigger machines were being invented. People from the countryside moved to the cities to work for long hours in big, dark, noisy factories.

Dickens himself worked in a factory for a short time when his father was in prison for debt. At eleven years old young Charles worked all day in a dark, cold room, sticking labels on bottles of boot polish. It was the most miserable time of his life. He grew up caring deeply about the poor, and especially the homeless, hungry and uneducated children of London.

In 1843 he thought of a Christmas story, *A Christmas Carol*. All that he believed about the need for the rich to help the poor and the importance of Christmas was poured into this book, which became a bestseller at once.

For the rest of his life, Dickens campaigned to help the poor. He died on 9 June 1870.